Fuzz, the Famous Fly

Written by Emily Rodda
Illustrated by Tom Jellett

An easy-to-read SOLO for beginning readers

Scholastic Canada Ltd.

New York Toronto London Auckland Sydney
Mexico City New Delhi Hong Kong

Scholastic Canada Ltd.
175 Hillmount Road, Markham, Ontario, Canada L6C 1Z7

Scholastic Inc.
555 Broadway, New York, NY 10012, USA

Scholastic Australia Pty Limited
PO Box 579, Gosford, NSW 2250, Australia

Scholastic New Zealand Limited
Private Bag 94407, Greenmount, Auckland, New Zealand

Scholastic Ltd.
Villiers House, Clarendon Avenue, Leamington Spa,
Warwickshire CV32 5PR, UK

Text copyright © Emily Rodda 1999.
Illustrations copyright © Tom Jellett 1999.

Cover design by Lyn Mitchell.
All rights reserved.

First published by Omnibus Books, part of the
SCHOLASTIC GROUP, Sydney, Australia.

National Library of Canada Cataloguing in Publication Data
Rodda, Emily
  Fuzz the famous fly
(Solo reading)
ISBN 0-439-98885-3
I. Jellett, Tom   II. Title.   III. Series.
PZ7.R6275Fu 2002   j813'.54   2001-900549-0

5 4 3 2 1   Printed and bound in Canada.   1 2 3 4 / 0

Chapter 1

Fuzz was very good-looking, for
a fly. His eyes sparkled like stars.
His wings were as shiny as rain
on broken glass. His legs were
long and thin, and he kept them
very clean.

He was also clever, and good at singing and dancing.

Fuzz lived in a small park with
his friends and family.

3

Their home was a cosy garbage can near a picnic bench. There was always lots of excellent garbage in the can, and it had a beautiful view of the gutter.

One morning, Fuzz was having breakfast – rotten hamburger with squashed banana on top – when some visitors came into the park and sat on the bench.

The man's shirt was the colour of
very old cheese. He was carrying
a camera.

The woman wore bright green clothes, and Fuzz could see that she had eaten toast and honey for breakfast. Crumbs were sticking to the front of her dress.

Fuzz loved toast and honey. He
was sure the woman didn't want
the crumbs. So he went and
helped himself.

The man lifted the camera, and
the woman smiled.

"That's nice," said Fuzz to himself. "She likes me." He did a little dance and buzzed a song in the woman's ear, to show that he liked her too.

The woman waved and clapped.
"Hold still," called the man, so
Fuzz did.

Click! The man took a picture.

Fuzz finished his toast and flew
away, not knowing that this day
was going to change his life.

Chapter 2

A few days later, the flies were having lunch – pizza mixed with peanut butter – when another visitor came into the park and sat on the bench.

He smelled wonderful, because he had stepped in something brown and sticky in the grass.

The visitor started to read the paper. All the flies went to look. They liked to see the news.

The man waved the paper
at them.

   "That's nice," Fuzz said.
"He's trying to show it to us."

Soon the man muttered, "Flies!" and went away, leaving the paper lying on the bench.

"You heard what he said," Fuzz told his friends. "He's left it for us to see."

They all buzzed down to look at the paper. And there, on the open page, was a picture of the woman in the green dress – and Fuzz!

"Look!" buzzed all the flies. "Fuzz! You're in the paper! You're famous!"

Fuzz felt so shy that he went pink, which for a fly is quite difficult.

But that was only the beginning.

Chapter 3

Word spread fast. Soon all the
flies in the park had seen the
paper. Lots of them asked for
Fuzz's autograph.

By lunch time, a fan club
had started.

Many visitors came to the park that day. The flies knew that they had come because they had seen Fuzz's picture in the paper.

Fuzz tried to say hello to everyone, so that no one felt left out. He danced and sang, too.

23

The visitors waved and clapped.
They loved him!

Fuzz was so busy that he hardly had time to eat. He missed at least six meals!

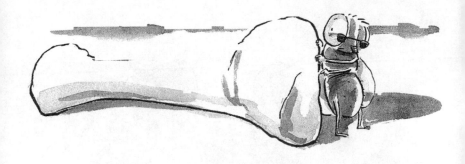

In the end, he had to rest. He put on sunglasses, so his fans wouldn't know him, and hid behind an old chicken bone.

The other flies came to visit him there. "Fuzz, you are a star," his wise old granny said. "You must leave home and share your talent with the world."

"Really?" said Fuzz. He was so excited that his tummy was flopping up and down. He ate some chicken, to settle it.

"Yes," agreed all the flies. "Fuzz, you are a star."

Fuzz felt very proud. "I'm a star," he said to himself.

He quickly packed a bag and
buzzed out of the garbage can.
A big car was waiting.

Fuzz took his place in the back seat. Then the car drove away.

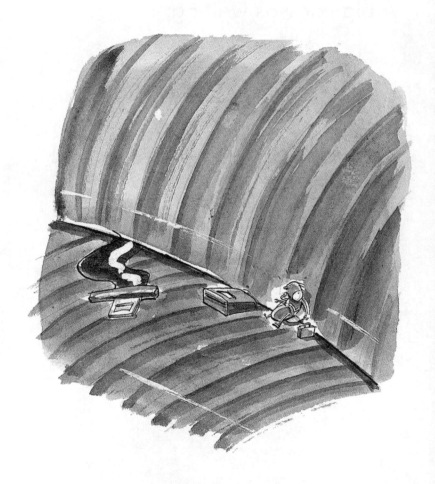

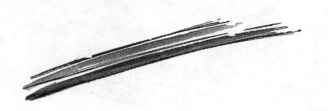

Fuzz pressed his nose against the window and watched until the little park was out of sight.

Chapter 4

Fuzz enjoyed life as a star.
Everyone he met was very nice to
him. They waved when they saw
him, and clapped when he sang
and danced. They loved him!

He worked hard. He was in ads and TV shows, and quite a few films.

His picture was often in the papers, too. He liked this best, because he knew that the flies at home would see the papers, and know he was OK.

He hoped they were proud of him. He hadn't seen them for a very long time. By now he had moved around the city so much that he no longer knew how to get back to the park.

Fuzz was famous. He ate the best food and drank the best drinks.

He drove in big cars, and slept in the richest garbage cans in the city.

But sometimes, late at night,
when he was alone, he felt sad.

"I know I'm lucky to be famous,"
he said to himself. "But I miss the
old flies at home."

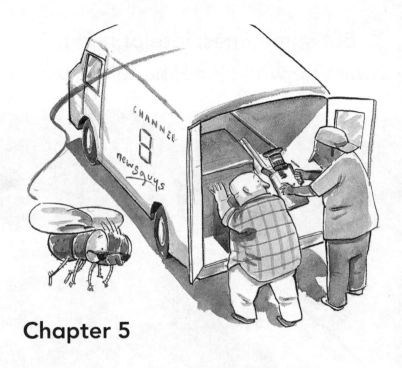

Chapter 5

One morning, Fuzz went to make
a TV ad about garbage. He knew
a lot about garbage, and was
glad to have the chance to tell
everyone how wonderful it was.

He had been to a big party the night before, and had stayed up late. He was tired when he crawled into the TV van.

"Sometimes, being a star is hard," he said to himself, as the van bumped along. He decided to have a little sleep.

He woke up when the van stopped.

"What a dump!" he heard one of the TV people say.

"This sounds like a nice place," said Fuzz to himself. He buzzed outside and looked around.

At first he didn't know where he was. And then, suddenly, his heart jumped.

It was his park! There was the gutter. There was the dear old can.

He was home!

"Fuzz! Oh, Fuzz!" His friends and family had seen him. They buzzed towards him. They crowded around him and hugged him.

"Flies!" said the TV people,
waving and clapping.

"I know," shouted Fuzz. "Isn't it
wonderful?"

"Oh, Fuzz, we have missed
you," his old granny cried.

"I've missed you too," said
Fuzz. "So much!"

When the TV people left that day, Fuzz didn't go with them. He was sorry to say goodbye. He knew they must be sorry, too. But he loved his old home too much to leave it, ever again.

And he never did.

When his fans came to the park,
he always sang and danced for
them. They waved and clapped,
so he knew they still loved him.

But every night, as he snuggled down in his cosy can, he felt very, very lucky.

"It's good to be famous," he said to himself. "But it's even better to be happy. And even for a famous fly like me, there's no place like home."

Emily Rodda

At home I have a photograph with a fly right in the middle of it. The fly sat on the camera lens while the picture was taken, just as though it wanted to be a star.

On TV you often see a fly buzzing around, if the show is about the outdoors. There have been flies in magazine pictures, too. I had always thought it was a different fly every time. Now I've started to wonder. Flies all look the same to us. But maybe there are special flies who try their hardest to be famous. Just like Fuzz.

Tom Jellett

I usually work next to an open window. This is great on a sunny day because a nice breeze blows in to cool me down. The problem is that the breeze also blows my drawings off the table, and I end up chasing them around the room!

Flies get in through my open window, too. They buzz all over the place, walk over my biscuits, fall into my cup of tea, and make real pests of themselves.

I tried to use these flies as models for my drawings of Fuzz and his friends, but I couldn't get them to sit still for a second!